Angelica
the Angel Fairy

Special thanks to
Mandy Archer

ORCHARD BOOKS
338 Euston Road, London NW1 3BH
Orchard Books Australia
Level 17/207 Kent Street, Sydney, NSW 2000
A Paperback Original

First published in 2012 by Orchard Books

HiT entertainment

A CIP catalogue record for this book is available
from the British Library.

ISBN 978 1 40831 688 7

1 3 5 7 9 10 8 6 4 2

Printed in Great Britain

The paper and board used in this paperback are natural recyclable
products made from wood grown in sustainable forests. The
manufacturing processes conform to the environmental regulations
of the country of origin.

Orchard Books is a division of Hachette Children's Books,
an Hachette UK company

www.hachette.co.uk

Angelica
the Angel Fairy

by Daisy Meadows

ORCHARD

www.rainbowmagic.co.uk

The Fairyland Palace

Seeing Pool

Tippington Town

Jack Frost's
Ice Castle

Village Hall

Throne
Room

Rachel's
House

Greenacre Rest Home

Tippington Children's Hospital

Jack Frost's Spell

Christmas angels shine and glitter,
But every year I grow more bitter.
Why does Santa only treat
Children who are kind and sweet?

Pretty gifts beneath the tree,
Those presents should belong to me!
Three magic objects in my fist
Will get my name on Santa's list.

The Sparkly
Pan Pipes

Contents

Christmas Chaos

"The Christmas fair opens in five minutes," said Rachel Walker, her eyes dancing with excitement. "Are we ready to turn on the fairy lights?"

"Definitely!" exclaimed her best friend, Kirsty Tate.

Kirsty was staying at Rachel's house for the first half of the school holidays.

The pair had enjoyed a wonderful, Christmassy week ice skating, drinking hot chocolates and baking gingerbread. Time always seemed to rush by when Kirsty and Rachel were together!

Now it was Saturday afternoon and the friends were dressed in their Brownie uniforms. The girls in Rachel's pack had been working hard all morning – today was the day of the Tippington Brownies' Christmas Fair! Kirsty and Rachel had volunteered to run the "winter woollies" stall, a tabletop stacked high with mittens, socks and scarves knitted in rich, festive colours.

Rachel ran to the back of the hall. When Brown Owl gave the signal, she dimmed the main lights.

Everyone closed their eyes in the

darkness and counted
down together. "Three,
two, one…go!"

Flash!

There was a thrilled
gasp, then an explosion
of clapping and
cheering. The Brownies
had transformed Tippington's plain old
village hall into a magical Christmas
grotto! Stalls lined every wall, each
one decorated with shiny green holly
sprigs, golden baubles and scarlet bows.
Garlands of glittery lights twinkled from
the ceiling. In the kitchen, Mrs Walker
and the other Brownie mums had
been busy brewing tea and plating up
Christmas treats, filling the air with the
smell of warm mince pies.

"Look at the tree." Rachel's mum beamed. "Isn't it magical?"

The girls had come in the day before to deck the hall's tree with candy canes, velvet ribbon and shimmering lantern-shaped lights. At the very top, Brown Owl had fixed a beautiful fairy in place.

14

Kirsty squeezed Rachel's hand and smiled. The friends knew a lot about fairies. From the very first day they met, the pair had been going on secret trips to Fairyland! They had shared some wonderful adventures with their magical friends. Both girls had made a secret promise to protect the fairies from Jack Frost and his grumpy goblins.

"Everybody to their positions, please," called Brown Owl. "It's time to open the doors."

There was an excited hustle and bustle as the Brownies rushed to their stalls.

"We should raise lots of money today," said Kirsty, hopefully. "Look at all these lovely things!"

This year, the Brownies had decided to celebrate the true spirit of Christmas.

Instead of splashing out on new equipment for the pack, they had chosen to buy gifts for people who weren't as lucky as they were. Giving to others was what Christmas was really all about.

"I can't wait to take a big sack of presents round to Tippington Children's Hospital." Kirsty smiled. "It must be miserable being poorly at this time of year."

Rachel ran over to help another Brownie called Claire unpack the last few baubles for her Christmas decorations stall.

"Don't forget

16

the rest home visit, too!" she called back.

The Brownies had voted to spend half of the money on gifts for the children's hospital and the other half on the residents of Greenacre Rest Home, which was just around the corner from Rachel's house.

"Smile everyone, please," trilled Brown Owl, unbolting the hall doors, "and Merry Christmas!"

Kirsty and Rachel swapped thrilled glances as the first shoppers trooped in from the cold. Soon there were customers milling up and down the aisles, picking up trinkets and treating themselves to yummy things to eat.

"You can be in charge of the money, Kirsty," suggested Rachel. "I'll put things in paper bags."

Both girls felt a bit nervous at first, but they soon got the hang of things. Before long, the hall was full of people. If the afternoon carried on like this, the fair would be a sell-out!

When the queue at their stall had calmed down a little, Kirsty slipped across to Claire's decoration table.

"Please could I have some change, Claire," she whispered. "Claire? Oh!"

Kirsty's face flushed. Instead of selling decorations, Claire was swishing a

piece of tinsel around.
Passing shoppers
had to duck out of
her way, but their
confused faces
only made the
Brownie burst
into cheeky
giggles.

"Look
at me!"
she giggled,
knocking a tray of
painted baubles onto the floor.

Kirsty knelt down to pick the
ornaments up. What *was* Claire doing?

Rachel rushed over to help.
"Something's wrong," she whispered.
"Come with me…"

An Old Fairy Friend

"Stand on this," said Rachel breathlessly, pulling a chair out from underneath the winter woollies table. "You'll get a better view."

Kirsty carefully climbed onto the chair and peered over the shoppers' heads.

"Everyone has abandoned their stalls!" She gasped. "And why is that Sixer munching mince pies? They're supposed to be for sale!"

Instead of serving their customers, Brownies were running up and down the aisles, calling each other names and shrieking with laughter.

"Look at the twins," said Rachel, pointing to the tombola on the stage.

Kirsty recognised Josie and Tilly from Rachel's last birthday party. Ten people were waiting patiently for a turn on the tombola, but the twins were ignoring them.

The naughty pair were far too busy plunging their hands into the ticket bucket and helping themselves to the best prizes.

22

"Every Brownie in the room is causing mischief," declared Kirsty. "At this rate we won't raise a penny!"

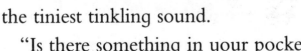

As she stepped down from the chair, Rachel heard the tiniest tinkling sound.

"Is there something in your pocket?" she asked.

Kirsty shook her head. Then the tinkling sound came again! It was a little louder this time, a delicate peal of silvery sleigh bells.

Rachel cupped
her hand to her ear.
There it was again!
Kirsty began to
gently lift up the
gloves and scarves on
the table, peeping hopefully
underneath each one. She felt sure
there must be a fairy nearby!

"Look at these," she whispered, holding
up a set of knitted pink mittens.

Rachel's heart fluttered. "The sound is
coming from inside!"

A stream of tiny musical notes
shimmered around one of the mittens.
The notes got brighter and brighter, until
a little fairy popped her head out! Kirsty
quickly turned the mitten round so no
one else could see.

"Hello again!" said the fairy. "Merry Christmas!"

Kirsty and Rachel beamed at each other. It was their old friend Melodie the Music Fairy. The last time they'd seen Melodie was at King Oberon and Queen Titania's spectacular 1000th jubilee celebrations.

"Merry Christmas!" Kirsty smiled.

"How lovely to see you," added Rachel, wondering if Melodie would know anything about the chaos at the Christmas Fair. "Is everything all right in Fairyland?"

Melodie climbed out
of the mitten and
smoothed down her
pretty pink dress.

"I'm afraid it's
not." She frowned.
"It's not all right
at all!"

She explained that a very special
musical instrument had been stolen from
the Fairyland Palace.

"We've lost a set of sparkly pan pipes.
They belong to my friend Angelica the
Angel Fairy, a wonderful Christmas
fairy who uses her magic to help us all
to be as good as we can be. Without
the sparkly pan pipes, fairies and
humans can't resist the temptation to be
naughty!" said Melodie.

"So that explains why the Brownies are behaving so badly," said Rachel. "Who could do such a thing at Christmas?"

"I bet I know," whispered Kirsty. "Jack Frost!"

Melodie stretched out her gorgeous pink wings and fluttered up to the window ledge.

"You're right!" She nodded, perching on the ledge. "But that's not the only thing he's taken. Angelica also looks after a snow-white feather and an enchanted name scroll. Santa Claus himself uses the scroll to work out who deserves presents each year.

Goodness knows what will happen on Christmas Eve if we don't get it back!"

"But that's only two days away!" cried Rachel. "We've got to do something!"

Kirsty agreed. "We can't waste a second."

Melodie's face lit up. "Oh, thank you!" She smiled, clapping her little hands. "Will you come with me to Fairyland? We can't let Jack Frost and his goblins spoil Christmas!"

"Of course," chorused the girls together.

Kirsty cupped the fairy in her hands, then followed Rachel to the Christmas tree. No one would be able to see them behind there! When they were ready, Melodie waved her wand and the enchanting sleigh-bell tune instantly began to play once more. She gently

touched each of the friends' heads with
the tip of her wand, pink notes popping
like glittering stars.

"Close your eyes," sang the fairy, her
little voice perfectly in tune with the music.

The girls felt themselves being swept up
and twirled high into the air. It was like
riding a magical merry-go-round!

Seeing Pool Secrets

Kirsty and Rachel opened their eyes to the most wonderful sight in the world. The best friends were hand in hand, sliding down a shimmering rainbow! The musical notes from Melodie's wand still sparkled and chimed all around them.

"We're fairies again!" whispered Kirsty excitedly.

Rachel wriggled her shoulders and smiled. A perfect pair of gossamer wings were gently uncurling on her back. As the rainbow arched down towards the clouds, she found herself flying along next to Melodie and Kirsty. The friends darted left and right, tumbling and twirling through the wintry sky.

Soon, red-and-white
toadstools came into
view below them,
dotted up and down
the snowy hillsides.
Rachel could even
see fairies fluttering
between the little homes!

She smiled and waved, but not one fairy
waved back.

"There's not much Christmas spirit
here today," explained Melodie. "Some
fairies are even refusing to tidy their
toadstools!"

"Oh my," answered Rachel. For a fairy
that really was very naughty indeed!
Without the sparkly pan pipes, everyone
was struggling to be their normal, helpful
selves.

The Music Fairy led the girls to the shining turrets of the Fairyland Palace.

"There's Angelica!" said Melodie, pointing to the Seeing Pool.

A lonely figure was perched on the edge of the pool, staring forlornly into its frozen surface. Her softly feathered wings drooped with sadness. The girls could see her sweet face reflected on the ice, framed by a tumble of auburn curls.

"H–hello," said Angelica, doing her very best to raise a smile. She was wearing a snow-white dress trimmed with swirling crystals. When the fairy stood up, her silk skirt swished gently around her.

"We came as soon as we heard," said Rachel. "We're sorry that Jack Frost's been up to no good again!"

Angelica's smile faded, her eyes brimming with silvery tears.

"Each one of my magical objects is truly precious." She sighed. "Especially at Christmas time!"

The girls listened carefully as Angelica explained the objects' special powers.

"The sparkly pan pipes bring peace, helping fairies and humans to be well-behaved. The snow-white feather is as pure as our hearts, a symbol of harmony that encourages us all to be gentle and kind."

"And the enchanted scroll?" asked Kirsty, her eyes filled with concern.

Angelica put her face in her hands. "That is the most precious of all! The enchanted scroll records the names of every fairy and child who has been good. I give the scroll to Santa every Christmas Eve before he loads up his sleigh."

Melodie put her arm round the Angel Fairy's shoulders.

"If Santa doesn't have his list of good children," Angelica added, "he won't know where to deliver his presents!"

Rachel remembered all the children staying in Tippington Hospital. Unless she and Kirsty could help Angelica, their Christmas wouldn't be happy or peaceful this year!

"Don't worry," she said. "We'll make

sure Jack Frost gives everything back."

Kirsty nodded, adding, "And before Christmas, too!"

Angelica's face filled with hope. "Melodie promised you would help. Thank you so much!"

At that very moment, a ray of sunlight passed over the Seeing Pool. A stunning golden firebird soared above the fairies' heads,  its plumes the colour of flames.

"Hey!" called a voice. "Wait for me!"

A fairy in a flowing orange dress glided down to join the group. It was Erin the Firebird Fairy, rushing to keep up with her best friend Giggles! As soon as she saw Kirsty and Rachel, Erin's face lit up.

"We've come to find Jack Frost," said Kirsty, "but we're not sure where to start."

"Why don't we ask the Seeing Pool?" suggested Erin, beckoning to Giggles.

The firebird touched the edge of the

pool with the tip of his tail feather and the ice instantly melted. The waters swirled, then parted to reveal a picture.

"Look!" cried Angelica.

Rachel peered into the pool and shivered. There was the Ice Lord in his castle, tooting noisily on the Angel Fairy's sparkly pan pipes! His goblin helpers hooted and laughed as he paraded up and down, blowing with all his might.

"Those pan pipes are fragile!" pointed out Melodie. "What if Jack Frost breaks them?"

"We mustn't let him," insisted Kirsty.

"We've got to go to the Ice Castle straight away," agreed Rachel. "Right this very second!"

Toot and Shout!

There was just time for Kirsty and Rachel to give Melodie and Erin a quick farewell hug before Angelica whisked them away to Jack Frost's Ice Castle.

The friends fluttered nervously above the castle's jagged towers, which stood cold and unwelcoming in the bitter breeze. Down below them, dozens of goblins were stomping noisily around the ramparts.

"This way!" cried Kirsty, pointing to a crooked turret on the far wing. It was dripping in icicles, each one diamond-sharp. The fairies darted into the tower through a cracked window.

"Toot-toot-tooooot!"

Inside, the tower echoed with the din of Jack Frost's rotten pipe-blowing. The fairies summoned up all their courage, then fluttered towards the terrible sound.

The flights of steps spiralled down and down, finally coming to a stop in front of a pair of huge iron doors. Two goblin guards stood in front, clasping their mitts over their big green ears.

"What a racket!" groaned one. "He's been hooting and tooting all morning!"

"When will it stop?" yelled the other, scrunching up his eyes.

The fairies pressed themselves against the cold stone wall.

"That's the throne room," whispered Rachel. "The next time the doors open, try and slip in behind the guards."

Angelica and Kirsty both nodded their heads.

Suddenly, a muffled voice started shouting from inside the throne room.

"Where are my new Christmas decorations?" barked Jack Frost. "Take this rubbish away!"

"Some people are never happy!" snivelled a goblin.

Suddenly the great doors creaked opened, giving the fairies the chance they needed. As the grumbling goblin scuttled out, Kirsty, Rachel and Angelica darted noiselessly into the hall. Jack Frost was standing in the centre of the chamber, shouting and stamping his foot.

A gaggle of goblins scowled and sulked
in the corner.

"I can see my sparkly pan pipes," said
Angelica in a hushed voice. "They're in
his hand!"

The fairies quickly hid themselves in
the dazzling ice chandelier that hung
over the throne. Kirsty perched herself on
a diamond droplet just above Jack Frost's
head.

"What has happened in here?" she
wondered, looking around.

The Throne Room had been decorated
for Christmas, but not in a way that
the girls had ever seen before. Instead of
brightening up the walls with tinsel and
holly wreaths, the goblins had strung
up spiderweb and thorns! In one corner
a spiky dead tree had been clumsily
propped up in an old bucket.

"Those pesky fairies say this instrument will make anyone well-behaved," snorted Jack Frost, tooting on the pan pipes as hard as he could. "What a load of rubbish! You goblins are even more useless than usual!"

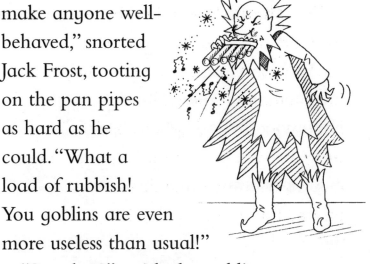

"So what?" smirked a goblin, shrugging his shoulders.

Jack Frost's face was white with rage.

"So what?" he bellowed. "I told you lot I wanted the finest Christmas decorations in the kingdom and what do I get? Mouldy webs and a tree that's no more than a dead twig!"

The dim-witted goblins looked over at the sorry Christmas tree, then burst into fits of laughter.

"Yeah!" sniggered one. "Bet there won't be many presents under that this year!"

Jack Frost kicked the tree so hard that it fell to the ground.

"That Angel Fairy lied!" he yelled furiously. "Those pan pipes simply don't work!"

Angelica couldn't stand to hear another word. The brave little fairy burst out of the chandelier, making the crystals ripple and chime.

"My pan pipes make people behave nicely," she said crossly, "not obey selfish commands!"

Pipes of Peace

"Angelica!" Kirsty cried out in dismay. "Be careful!"

Rachel reached for her friend's hand. "We have to help her."

Angelica fluttered left and right, still trying to reason with the furious Ice Lord.

"I would never tell a lie," she said earnestly. "The sparkly pan pipes will only work if you play them properly."

"Tooot-toot-tooot!"

Rachel watched in astonishment.
Jack Frost
wasn't
listening to
a word that
Angelica was
saying!

"He still hasn't
seen her," she gasped.
"He's too busy
shouting and making
that dreadful noise!"

The friends darted behind the frozen throne. In between blasting out-of-tune toots on the pan pipes, Jack Frost continued to bark and bellow at his foolish servants. The cheeky goblins weren't in the mood for grovelling,

and they argued back just as loudly. Not
one of them stopped to notice the tiny
fairy pleading to be heard. At last, poor
Angelica had to give up.

"He thought the pan pipes would
make the goblins obey his every
command," she told her friends, "but
they're being even naughtier than usual!"

Kirsty looked
thoughtful for a
moment, before
starting to smile.
She'd just had a
brilliant idea!

"I know how
to get Jack Frost's
attention," she said,
"but it's not going to be
easy."

53

Rachel and Angelica listened intently as their friend proposed that they each used their hands to block the ends of the sparkly pan pipes. Kirsty had counted that the magical instrument had six pipes tied together with silver thread – one for each fairy hand! The difficult part would be flying close enough to Jack Frost without getting batted away or even worse, caught!

"If he hears that his plan won't work, he might be persuaded to give the pan pipes back," said Rachel hopefully.

Angelica nodded. "It's worth a try."

The threesome fluttered out into the middle of the Throne Room.

"You goblins had better sort that tree out or I'll…I'll…What's that?" Jack Frost scowled. "Fairies in my Ice Castle?"

Kirsty and Rachel darted to one side,
just missing a flick from the Ice Lord's
bony finger. Angelica whirled round
the other way, grasping the end of the
sparkly pan pipes
with both hands.

Jack Frost
lifted the
enchanted
instrument
to his lips,
with the
Angel Fairy still
clinging on.

"I'll show you!" he
roared, blowing as hard as he could.

"Come on, Rachel!" shouted Kirsty,
flying up to put her hands over two more
holes.

Jack Frost swung the pan pipes from side to side, but Kirsty and Angelica held on tight.

"Nearly there!" puffed Rachel, flitting from left to right.

At last she managed to flutter in and clutch on to the last two pipes. The furious hooting and tooting stopped at once. Jack gasped in surprise.

"Well done, girls!" said Angelica with a proud smile. She flew up to face Jack Frost. "Now, if you'd just listen, I can tell you exactly why the pan pipes aren't working."

The Ice Lord
waited sulkily
as the little
Angel Fairy
had her say.
When he
realised that
she was telling
the truth his mouth
twisted into a scowl.

"Will you give the sparkly pan pipes
back now?" demanded Rachel. "They're
no use to you."

Jack Frost replied with a rude "Pah!"
and tossed the precious object to the
floor. Angelica dashed down to catch it.

"Watch out!" pleaded Kirsty. A clumsy
goblin was lifting up his enormous foot
at just the wrong moment!

The Angel Fairy touched the pan pipes with the tip of her wand in the nick of time. A cascade of golden stars whirled around the magical object, shrinking it down to fairy-size. Angelica tucked the pipes under her arm, then fluttered back to join her friends.

"Let's get you back to Tippington," she said, breathlessly. "They'll be needing you at the Christmas Fair!"

Despite its sorry start, the Brownie sale was going strong. Jolly shoppers strolled up and down the aisles, chatting with friends and neighbours. Brown Owl stood proudly in front of the tree, watching her girls happily serve the queues of shoppers.

"It's just delightful," cooed Angelica, "so Christmassy!"

"Will you stay for a while?" asked Rachel, finding a cosy hiding spot for the fairy on the winter woollies stall.

"I'd love to," replied Angelica. "Without

you, Jack Frost would still have the enchanted pan pipes!"

The little fairy lifted the magical instrument to her lips. As she started to play a beautiful Christmas carol, people began to gather round Kirsty and Rachel's stall.

"Look out of the window," whispered Rachel to her friend.

Kirsty looked, and her face shone with happiness. Outside the hall, the first snowflakes of winter were gently starting to fall.

"I've got a feeling that this is going to be our most successful Brownie Fair ever!" Kirsty beamed. "Merry Christmas!"

The Snow-White Feather

Contents

Sunshine and Snowflakes

"I love snow!" declared Kirsty, cupping a handful in her gloves and shaping it into a snowball.

"At Christmas time it's *extra*-special," added Rachel. "Tippington has turned into a winter wonderland!"

She giggled as Kirsty sent the snowball tumbling through the air. It disappeared into a holly bush dotted with scarlet berries, making the leaves rustle and sparkle in the light.

It really was a beautiful day to be
outside. A steady layer of snowflakes
had been falling silently ever since the
Brownie sale. The town's white paths and
rooftops twinkled brightly like a picture
from a pretty Christmas card.

Kirsty slipped an arm through Rachel's.
"It all started with Angelica's visit,"
she whispered, thinking of the new fairy
friend they had met the day before.

Rachel nodded enthusiastically. The
golden sunbeams dancing on the snow
reminded her of Angelica the Angel
Fairy's tumbling auburn curls.

The girls trudged on through the
snowy streets, taking in the magic. Kirsty,
Rachel and all the other Brownies were
on their way to deliver Christmas gifts
to the residents of Greenacre Rest Home.

Under their snuggly coats everyone was dressed smartly in their uniforms, their hair tied back with glittery lengths of tinsel.

"We're here, Kirsty!" said Rachel, pointing to a large Victorian house at the end of a sweeping drive.

Brown Owl led the pack up the drive. A beautiful Christmas wreath twinkled above the front door.

"I can't wait to see
the residents' faces
when they spot our
baskets of goodies,"
beamed Kirsty, her
cheeks rosy with cold.

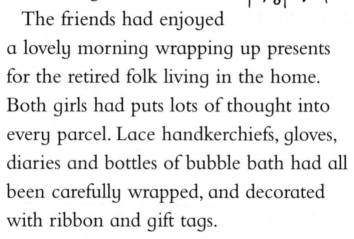

The friends had enjoyed
a lovely morning wrapping up presents
for the retired folk living in the home.
Both girls had puts lots of thought into
every parcel. Lace handkerchiefs, gloves,
diaries and bottles of bubble bath had all
been carefully wrapped, and decorated
with ribbon and gift tags.

The Brownies waited patiently,
stamping their feet in the snow. At last
the door swung open and a lady with a
smiley face stepped out to greet them.

"Welcome!" she called in a jolly voice.

The lady introduced herself as Mrs Pepper, the owner of the rest home. She led the girls into the porch and showed them where to hang their coats.

"Can you hear that?" whispered Kirsty, as soon as they got inside.

Rachel listened for a moment. The muffled sound of Christmas carols echoed down the hallway.

"The residents are listening to music in the day room," explained Mrs Pepper. "The old records are their favourites!"

Mrs Pepper showed the Brownies into a cosy sitting room, which had a fire roaring in the grate. A group of ladies and gentlemen were sat in a semi-circle around a record player, listening to a bright festive tune.

"Hello!" said Rachel brightly, eager to meet everyone.

A grey-haired fellow scowled at her, then hid behind his newspaper.

Kirsty knelt down beside an old lady in a flowery dress.

"My favourite carol is *Silent Night*," she said. "What's yours?"

The old lady glared at Kirsty, then harrumphed very loudly and turned to face the window.

Kirsty and Rachel glanced at each other in surprise. This wasn't the welcome they had been expecting!

"Come on," suggested Kirsty in a low voice, "let's put the presents under the tree."

The girls quietly started to unpack the gifts from their baskets and stack them under the Christmas tree in the corner.

"Hey, you!" called a voice.

"Yes?" asked Rachel, leaping up with a smile.

A tiny old lady wearing a pair of glasses on a chain scowled back at her.

"Can you move?" she snapped. "I can't see the tree with your big head in the way!"

Before poor Rachel could think of an answer, another lady pulled herself up to her feet.

"Edith Smythe!" she bellowed. "You're wearing my specs!"

"Well, they're mine now!" insisted Mrs Smythe.

The lady made a swipe for the glasses chain, but Mrs Smythe batted her hand out of the way. The Brownies watched in stunned silence as the pair began to make faces and call each other names.

Other residents started to join in the ruckus, too. A gentleman in a green cardigan snatched his neighbour's hearing aid, then three old ladies began to squabble about who had the best chair. The shouting got so loud it was even drowning out the record player's Christmassy music. Instead of behaving like grans and granddads, the old people were acting like grumpy toddlers!

An Unexpected Visitor

"There's not much Christmas spirit in here," frowned Kirsty. "I wouldn't be surprised if Jack Frost isn't making mischief again."

Rachel nodded urgently. She had been thinking the exact same thing!

"This has got to stop," she agreed, rushing over to the record player and lifting up the needle. If she could just get the residents' attention, she might be able to persuade them to calm down and be kind to each other!

The vinyl record stopped spinning, but somehow the carol kept on playing.

"Look," gasped Rachel in astonishment, "it must be fairy magic!"

Kirsty's heart skipped a beat. The merry festive tune still echoed through the speakers. Every time the chorus hit a high note, a tiny golden star appeared. Each star glittered for a moment, before shimmering out of sight.

"Those stars are getting brighter," remarked Rachel, standing in front of the speakers to hide the twinkling lights. The room was in such a terrible commotion, nobody even noticed.

78

The stars began to fizz even more brilliantly. Suddenly a flash of gold swished past the friends so fast it made them blink.

"Oh!" gasped a tinkly voice. "It's even worse than I thought!"

Kirsty and Rachel opened their eyes at once. There was Angelica the Angel Fairy, fluttering in the air in front of them!

In an instant the little fairy was gone again, darting across to the Christmas tree. She tucked herself in amongst the thick pine branches at the back, then beckoned for the girls to come over.

79

Kirsty and Rachel put the record back on, then rushed over to the tree.

"It's the snow-white feather, isn't it?" whispered Kirsty, crouching down. "Everyone here is being ever so mean!"

"Yes." Angelica nodded. "I came as soon as I heard."

The fairy's little heart-shaped face looked pale with worry. She explained how she'd just met Gabriella the Snow Kingdom Fairy flying over the hills of Fairyland.

"Gabriella warned me that she'd spotted a mob of goblins heading to the human world," she sighed. "So I decided to follow them. I knew they would be up to no good! Ever since we rescued the sparkly pan pipes from Jack Frost's Ice Castle he's been trying to find somewhere to hide the other magical objects."

"So did the goblins lead you here?" said Rachel.

"That's right," said Angelica breathlessly. "They've got to be somewhere inside Greenacre."

"Ach-oo!"

Kirsty and Rachel sprang to their feet. A rather curious-looking care worker in a green uniform wobbled into the day room, pushing a clanking tea trolley.

"ACH-OO!"

The care worker sneezed again, barging his way through the Brownies and residents. The very loud sneeze matched the stranger's very large nose. An old lady put down her knitting and demanded a cup of tea, but the care worker completely ignored her.

"Look what he's doing," gasped Rachel, her eyes wide with shock.

Instead of serving drinks, the worker leant across the trolley and yanked the top off the biscuit tin. He began to shove handfuls of digestives into his mouth, gobbling down three at a time.

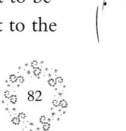

"Isn't he meant to be passing those out to the

residents?" said Kirsty.

Angelica fluttered out from behind a fairy light.

"We've found our first goblin," she announced, her eyes dancing with excitement.

Rachel and Kirsty edged a little closer. Milk and tea were splattered all over the trolley, but they couldn't see the snow-white feather anywhere. When the greedy goblin had shoved every last biscuit into his mouth, he began to push his way back out of the door. There was only one thing to do.

"Follow that goblin!" the girls chimed together.

A Thousand Feathers!

Kirsty pointed to the golden piece of tinsel tied around Rachel's blonde ponytail.

"Angelica," she said urgently, "do you think you can hide yourself at the back of Rachel's hair? The bow should cover you."

Angelica gave her wand a bold little wave to show that she was ready. The girls carefully helped the tiny fairy to wriggle in between the loops of tinsel wrapped round Rachel's ponytail. She tucked herself in so beautifully, even Kirsty had a hard job spotting her.

"Let's go!" called Angelica in a tinkly voice no louder than a whisper.

The friends picked their way across the room, stepping in between the angry residents and flustered Brownies.

"Hurry!" urged Rachel, slipping out of the door just before Brown Owl and Mrs Pepper wandered inside.

86

Further down the hallway, the wheels on the tea trolley rattled and squeaked. Kirsty and Rachel ran after it, ducking into doorways whenever the goblin stopped to sneeze or scratch his nose. Suddenly a loud *bang!* echoed down the corridor.

Angelica pushed her head out of the tinsel and stretched her wings.

"He's gone into that storeroom and slammed the door!" she cried, anxiously looping the loop. Butterflies flipped in Kirsty's tummy. She took a deep breath, then grabbed the handle firmly and gave it a twist.

"Oh!" cried Kirsty.

The storeroom door swung open to reveal not one, not two, but *three* goblins! Jack Frost's naughty servants were larking about with the care home's medical equipment, hooting with cheeky laughter. The first goblin had pulled off his care worker's uniform and was now picking up bandages and lobbing them at his friends' heads. Another one was making a terrible din as he raced round and round in a wheelchair. He skidded and screeched into chairs and cabinets, guffawing loudly at every crash.

"The snow-white feather can't be in here," Angelica whispered in dismay. "Those goblins are being far too thoughtless!"

"What's happening in the corner?" gasped Kirsty, staring at a goblin with pointy ears.

The mischievous creature barged through a row of walking frames, knocking them in all directions. He began to stack the frames clumsily, one on top of another, and clamber up. The tower wobbled and swayed with the goblin's weight.

"Bet I can reach the ceiling!" he yelled, blowing a raspberry.

"Those frames are going to get bent if he carries on like that!" said Rachel, putting her hands on her hips. She stepped into the storeroom, then coughed loudly. "A-hem!"

The goblin with the pointy ears jumped so high he banged his head on the ceiling! The whole stack of frames clattered down to the floor, causing a dreadful racket.

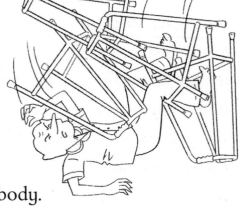

"Owwww!" he groaned, heaving the frames off his body.

His two friends yanked him up by the arms. They'd already spotted Angelica fluttering in the doorway!

"Get up!" yelled the first goblin. "We've got to get out of here!"

The second goblin elbowed his way through the door.

"Trust a pesky fairy to spoil our fun," he muttered, swiping at Angelica as he barged down the corridor. The little fairy darted out of reach, leaving a trail of golden swirls shimmering in the air behind her.

"Are you all right?" asked Rachel, when the goblins had passed.

"Yes, thank you!" trilled Angelica. "Well done for interrupting those troublemakers, that was really brave!"

Kirsty gave her best friend's hand a proud squeeze.

"This way!" Angelica cried. "They're heading towards the bedrooms."

The girls hurried along the corridor just a few metres behind the stomping goblins. The silly threesome pushed and

92

shoved each other to get to the front, knocking into pictures and bashing against doors. The goblins argued loudly all the way, not giving a hoot about the commotion they were making.

Soon the goblin with the pointy ears couldn't help boasting again.

"I'm the best climber *and* I'm the best hider too!" he teased, pulling faces at the others.

The first goblin scratched his head,
asking, "What do you mean?"

"I found the perfect place for that
magic feather," he bragged. "Take a look
in here!"

The goblin threw open a bedroom door
and ushered his mates inside. Angelica
and her friends slipped in behind them,
their hearts racing with
excitement.

"Oh no!" cried
Kirsty.

The bedroom
was filled with
even more
goblins, whacking
and walloping
each other in an
enormous pillow fight!

Jack Frost's daft servants were thumping each other so hard that the pillows were bursting. Feathers tumbled and swirled in every direction.

Silvery tears sprang to Angelica's eyes.

"There must be a thousand snow-white feathers in here," she exclaimed. "Which one is mine?"

Mischief and Mayhem

It was a truly shocking sight. Soft white
feathers floated and curled around the
room like a swirling snowstorm. A pair of
goblins jumped up and down on the bed,
taking swipes with pillows at their mates
on the floor. Another swung from the
lightshade, knocking other goblins over
with his enormous green feet.

Angelica fluttered to the dressing table then signalled for Kirsty and Rachel to tiptoe along the wall and duck down beside her.

"What do we do now?" asked the fairy. Finding one special feather amongst all this mayhem would be impossible!

The goblin with the pointy ears didn't seem too pleased either.

"Oh, rubbish!" he barked. "You pests have messed up my hiding place."

His mate chuckled with glee.

"What's Jack Frost going to say?" he taunted. "Bet he won't be so proud of you now, eh?"

The pointy-eared goblin prodded him in the chest.

"Shut up!" he yelled. "I stashed it in the bottom pillow in the corner. How was I to know that this lot would come in and muddle everything up? You'd better help me look or we'll all be in trouble."

The anxious goblin began to pick up pillows one by one, turning them upside down and shaking the cases until feathers settled all over the carpet. His mate reluctantly lent a hand.

"Not in this one," he muttered, "or this, or this."

Rachel shook her head at the foolish pair.

"Now there are even *more* feathers flying around the room," she said.

"We'd better start looking too," said Kirsty, picking up a pillowcase and peeping inside. "What else can we do?"

Angelica's little voice began to tremble.

"What about all these goblins?" she asked nervously.

"If we stay in the corner we should be all right," said Rachel, gently. "Most of them are too busy fighting to notice us."

The friends started searching. Kirsty and Rachel sifted through handfuls of feathers, hoping to spot one that stood out from the rest. Angelica danced around like a golden sunbeam, her lovely curls bobbing as she flew. They looked and looked until their eyes got tired, but the enchanted snow-white feather was nowhere to be seen.

On the other side of the bedroom, the goblin with the pointy ears had already given up.

"This is a waste of time," he grumbled. "Trust you lot!"

"Don't blame me!" bellowed the goblin next to him, bopping him on the nose with his half-stuffed pillow.

The pointy-
eared goblin
made a
lunge for
the pillow,
then hit
his rival on
the bottom.
It was such a
perfect shot that
the goblins on the bed
stopped to clap.

"Go on, get him back!" they whooped, their eyes gleaming.

The pair didn't need telling twice. They were soon thumping and walloping each other with such force that a new flurry of feathers tumbled to the floor.

Angelica squealed with delight.

"There it is!"

One snow-white plume shimmered as it fell silently to the ground. A haze of silver fairy dust twinkled all around it, glittering like crystals.

Kirsty and Rachel scrambled to catch the feather, but the pointy-eared goblin got there first.

"I'll have that!" he roared, seizing the precious object in his big green hands.

Christmas Spirit

"Be careful!" wailed Rachel, as the goblin's fingers closed around Angelica's treasured possession. "The snow-white feather is very delicate!"

Kirsty stepped forward to support her friend, adding, "And it doesn't belong to you!"

"You again?" grunted the goblin. "Get lost!"

The smug creature lifted his arms up above the girls' heads so they couldn't reach the feather. Angelica flitted after it, then perched precariously on his thumb.

"Please let go," she begged, desperately trying to unpeel the goblin's fingers.

The pointy-eared goblin tried to gloat at the fairy, but his sneer didn't come out quite right. The other pillow-fighters nudged each other. The goblin's face was beginning to relax into a calm smile.

"That's the magic

of the snow-white feather," Angelica explained gently. "It makes everyone kind and gentle – *even* grumpy old goblins!"

Kirsty and Rachel's eyes lit up. No wonder this magical object was so precious at Christmas time!

The little Angel Fairy tapped the goblin's hand with her wand.

"Excuse me," she said quietly. "May I have my feather back, please?"

The goblin nodded his head and politely bowed to Angelica. Rachel had to stifle a giggle.

"I've never seen such good goblin behaviour," she whispered to Kirsty.

Her best friend beamed. Jack Frost would not be impressed at all! The goblin graciously opened his palm. Angelica gave the snow-white feather the slightest touch with the tip of her golden wand. In an instant it had shrunk back down to fairy-size.

"That's better," she cooed, holding the tiny plume between her finger and thumb.

The delighted fairy twirled back to her friends, her cheeks flushed with pleasure.

"That was a surprise," grinned Kirsty, "for everyone!"

The pointy-eared goblin's eyes were as wide as saucers. He was still standing with his hand outstretched, wondering where his feather had gone! As soon as the magical object was out of his grasp, his naughty goblin streak returned.

"Did I just do what I think I did?" he wailed.

His mates grabbed the unfortunate goblin by the neck, then dragged him towards the door.

"Yes, you did!" grumbled the first goblin, shaking his head in disappointment.

"What did you go and do that for?" snapped the other one. "The boss will be hopping mad when he hears you've been helping pesky fairies."

The pointy-eared goblin screwed up his face.

"Helping fairies?" he howled. "I've never been so ashamed!"

The rest of the goblin mob dropped their pillows and made a run for it. They wanted to get back to the Ice Castle before Jack Frost heard the bad news!

110

The hapless servants jostled and shoved their way past the girls, slamming the door behind them.

"Phew," breathed Rachel, when the coast was clear. "That's one way to frighten off a goblin!"

Angelica burst into a peal of fairy giggles.

"Thank you so much, girls," she beamed. "His face was a funny sight."

It was time
for the
Angel Fairy
to take the
snow-white
feather back
to Fairyland,
but she had
one last job to
do first. Angelica
waved her wand
with a little
flourish.

"How pretty!" sighed Kirsty, as a stream
of twinkly fairy dust swirled around the
room. When the sparkles had settled, all
the pillows were plumped up and back
on the beds again. There wasn't a stray
feather in sight!

Kirsty and Rachel waved goodbye to Angelica, then made their way back to Greenacre's day room.

"It's even better than we could have wished for," gushed Rachel, peeping inside.

"Deck the halls with boughs of holly, fa la la la la la la la la!"

Now that the snow-white feather was out of goblin hands, the home's residents had stopped arguing and fighting. Instead

they were gathered around the tree,
listening to the Brownies singing their
favourite Christmas carols. Mrs Pepper
and Brown Owl stood by the fire, their
faces flushed with pleasure.

Kirsty and Rachel took their places in the group and joined in with the singing.

"It really is the season to be jolly, isn't it?" whispered Kirsty.

Rachel agreed. Everyone was having a magical time! The fun had only just begun, too. As the last chorus trailed off, the excited Brownies made their way towards the Christmas tree.

"Come on, Kirsty," exclaimed Rachel. "Let's hand out those presents!"

The Enchanted Name Scroll

Contents

Christmas Countdown

"So what have you put on your Christmas list, Billy?" asked Kirsty, perching on the end of a hospital bed.

A little boy in dinosaur pyjamas clapped his hands with excitement.

"A Tyrannosaurus rex!" he announced. "A really big one!"

Rachel's eyes twinkled with mischief. "Have you been good this year?"

Billy nodded proudly. It was the night before Christmas and Rachel's Brownie pack had come to visit the patients at Tippington Children's Hospital. The corridors looked cosy and bright, covered from floor to ceiling in jolly decorations and fairy lights. Doctors wandered up and down in Santa hats, checking charts and handing out medicine. Garlands of tinsel sparkled around the nurses' stations and festive tunes echoed down the wards.

"What a magical way to spend Christmas Eve," whispered Kirsty. "This time of year is all about sharing, isn't it?"

"That's right," agreed Rachel. "I can't wait to see the children's faces when they see what we've brought!"

Rachel pulled a little pencil and notebook out of her uniform pocket, then

wrote down Billy's name. The Brownie pack had used the money raised at the Christmas Fair to buy toys for the boys and girls who were too poorly to go home for the holidays. Now the Brownies needed to make sure that each patient got something that they would like to play with. The hospital day room was stacked with trains and cars, teddies and tea sets. Each toy had been carefully wrapped up in bright paper and tied with curly ribbon.

"Do you remember the plastic dinosaur with the green tail?" asked Kirsty. "That would be a perfect present for Billy!"

Rachel ticked the toy creature off her list, then slipped the notebook back in her pocket.

"Merry Christmas!" she grinned, wandering over to say hello to a small girl with a leg raised up in a plaster cast.

"I'm Emily," replied the girl in a shy voice. "I broke my leg ice-skating."

Kirsty gave Emily's hand a friendly squeeze.

"You poor thing," she smiled. "Maybe

Santa will bring you something extra-special this year!"

Instead of smiling back, the little patient's eyes suddenly glistened with tears.

"How is he going to know where to deliver the presents?" she asked. "I didn't think I'd be in *here* on Christmas morning."

"Santa never gets things wrong," replied Rachel. "He's got a special list."

"I hope so," sighed Emily, sinking back on her pillows. "I don't know what I'd do if Santa forgot me on Christmas Eve."

Rachel tried to sound cheery, but inside her heart gave a little flutter. She wondered what would happen if Angelica's enchanted name scroll wasn't found before bedtime.

Kirsty looked worried, too. There were only hours to go before Santa Claus would be leaving his workshop at the North Pole. Although Angelica had two of her magical objects back, Jack Frost was still hiding the fairy's precious scroll. The scroll contained the names of all the children who had been good. If Angelica didn't give the scroll to Santa, he wouldn't know where to deliver his presents.

"What did you wish for?" asked Kirsty, taking a quick peep out of the hospital window. Outside the sky was already dark. Snowflakes fell silently over the town.

Emily's eyes shone hopefully.

"I'd love a toy fairy," she gushed, "to play make-believe with."

126

Just then, a nurse
in navy trousers
wheeled a food trolley
onto the ward. On her
tunic a Christmas tree
brooch flashed merrily
next to a name badge
saying 'Sally'.

"Tea time!" called
Nurse Sally. "Who fancies a
sandwich and a slice of chocolate Yule
log?"

While Brown Owl and the rest of the
pack helped pass around the trays of
food, Kirsty led Rachel a little way up
the corridor.

"We can't let Emily and the others
down," she whispered. "We've got to find
the enchanted name scroll. It's nearly

time for Santa to load up his sleigh."

Rachel agreed. "I'd hoped it would have turned up by now. I can't even think where to start looking."

Just then, three hospital porters in white coats tumbled out of a side room. They marched towards Rachel and Kirsty, their eyes fixed on the floor. *Bash!* The clumsy trio knocked straight into Nurse Sally's food trolley. The nurse gasped as the trolley was sent rolling down the corridor.

"Careful!" frowned Rachel, running over to help. The friends caught the food trolley just in time, but the porters didn't even bother to say sorry.

"What are you three doing here anyway?" demanded Nurse Sally, putting her hands on her hips. "I didn't call for a porter!"

The curious workers muttered something under their breath. Then the tallest one broke into an awkward run, pushing past Rachel as he bolted for the door.

Rachel shivered.

"That was Jack Frost," she gasped. "He's here!"

A Flicker of Fairy Magic

"Are you sure it was Jack Frost?"
whispered Kirsty.

"Certain," insisted Rachel. "He was
freezing cold. I bet he's brought a couple
of goblins with him, too!"

Kirsty wheeled the trolley back into
the middle of the ward. As soon as Nurse
Sally and the Brownies were busy again
giving out the children's teas, the girls
made a dash for it. If Jack Frost was

lurking in Tippington Children's Hospital, they needed to find him fast! The girls tiptoed past the nurses' station then pushed through the ward's double doors.

"There he is!" exclaimed Kirsty.

Now they were out of the grown-ups' sight, Jack Frost and his goblins didn't even bother to try and disguise themselves. Their big clumpy feet clattered down the corridor, making a terrible racket. The threesome bumped and jostled all the way, eyeing each other with grumpy faces.

"Come on!" yelled Jack Frost, tugging the nearest goblin by the collar. "Santa won't wait much longer!"

The Ice Lord dug a hand into his coat pocket and pulled out a golden roll of parchment tied with a red velvet ribbon.

Kirsty and Rachel both gasped in surprise. It had to be Angelica's enchanted name scroll! Before the girls could get any closer, a doctor strolled down the corridor. Quick as a flash, Jack Frost ducked into an empty side bay.

"Where'd he go?" gawped one of the goblins, wrinkling his wonky nose.

133

The other goblin scratched his head.
"Don't ask me!"

The doctor stared at the daft pair. Just
when it looked as though
he was going to say
something, an icy
hand reached
out of the
side bay and
dragged the
goblins inside.
The door
slammed shut
behind them.
The doctor
shrugged, then smiled
at Kirsty and Rachel. As soon as he had
passed, the girls rushed up to the side
bay and peered through the window.

Inside they could see Jack Frost and his goblins huddled in a corner. All three were talking in urgent voices, pointing and glaring at the enchanted scroll.

"They're definitely up to no good," Rachel frowned. "We can't let them do anything to spoil Santa's list!"

As she spoke, the string of fairy lights on the wall above her seemed to flare even brighter.

"We're going to have to go in there," decided Kirsty, pushing against the door.

Rachel caught her friend's arm. There was no doubt about it – the lights were twinkling faster now, too!

"I wonder," she said in a hushed voice. "Could Angelica be close by?"

The girls held hands – both wishing and hoping for fairy magic.

A glittering swoosh of gold burst out from the lights, sending sparkles spiralling in all directions. Angelica the Angel Fairy fluttered into view, a tiny trail of fairy dust cascading behind her. Her cheeks had flushed the colour of pink rosebuds.

"Kirsty! Rachel!" she exclaimed. "I
didn't think I'd get here in time!"

The friends said a quick hello, thrilled
to be together again.

"The scroll is in there…" whispered
Rachel urgently,
keeping her voice
as low as she
could.

"…in Jack
Frost's hands!"
finished Kirsty.

Angelica gave
a little gasp. "As
soon as I heard
that Jack Frost was

on his way to the human
world, I decided to follow him,"
she announced in a brave voice. "What

can he be doing in a children's hospital?"

A noisy shout rang out from the side bay.

"This piece of paper is useless," bellowed Jack Frost, "just like you goblins!"

"Watch out!" gasped Kirsty, pulling Rachel back from the door.

The door swung back on its hinges with a deafening thud. Angelica darted up into the fairy lights just as Jack Frost came thundering into view. Kirsty and Rachel pressed themselves against the wall.

The two goblins lolloped into the corridor, too. They craned their heads left and right, but the foolish pair didn't think to look behind them!

"Get me a pen, NOW!" barked Jack

Frost. "My name needs to be scrawled on that list in the biggest letters Santa's ever seen!"

The Name Game

As soon as Jack Frost and his silly servants had crashed back down the corridor, Rachel stood up on her tiptoes.

"Angelica," she called gently. "It's safe to come out now."

The little fairy flitted out of her hiding spot.

"We need to get closer to Jack Frost," she decided. "It sounds as if he is about to do something very selfish indeed."

Rachel felt a little frightened at the thought of eavesdropping on Jack Frost — what would happen if they got caught?

"It's not going to be easy," agreed Kirsty. "These long corridors don't have many hiding places when you're our size."

The Angel Fairy gave her wand the tiniest tap.

"How would you like to be fairies again?" she asked.

Both girls shared a delighted smile.

"Oh, yes please," replied Rachel. "That would make things much easier!"

Angelica twirled her wand in a circle, sending a cloud of fairy dust dancing in all directions. The friends watched in delight as the sprinkles began to settle

in their hair. Rachel took a deep breath.
The fairy dust smelled of everything
she loved about Christmas – pine trees,
gingerbread and candy canes all rolled
into one!

"I can feel myself shrinking!" declared
Kirsty, as a glistening
pair of wings
magically
appeared
on her
back. The
delicate
pink
wings
were so
pale she
could almost
see through them.

Rachel twitched her shoulders and felt her own wings begin to open and close gently.

"Isn't it wonderful?" she marvelled.

The friends could have tumbled and twirled through the air all day, but they didn't dare waste another second. They flew straight up to Angelica's side and listened carefully to her instructions.

"Follow me down the corridor," said the Angel Fairy. "Try and fly as high as you can. If we stay close to the Christmas decorations, Jack Frost shouldn't notice us."

"Good idea," agreed Kirsty.

One by one the fairies flitted down the corridor, darting in and out of the paper chains and tinsel.

It didn't take long to track down Jack Frost and his goblins. The naughty threesome had wandered into a ward that had been closed for the Christmas break. The three stood at the end of an empty hospital bed, hunched over the mattress.

"Oh my!" gasped Angelica, in a voice no louder than the ting of a triangle.

Rachel and Kirsty fluttered down and perched on the head of the bedframe. The naughty goblins had stretched the enchanted scroll out so that Jack Frost could write his name at the top! The Ice Lord tried again and again to make a mark on the magical parchment, but nothing seemed to work.

"I need another pen!" he growled. "Now!"

The goblin with the wonky nose rolled his eyes.

"We've given you dozens already," he grumbled. "Felt-tips, ballpoints, markers — you've had the lot!"

The other goblin groaned. "You've been scribbling on that scroll ever since you pinched it from Fairyland. Can't we just go back to the Ice Castle?"

Jack Frost threw the pen on the floor.

"Silence!" he ordered. "I need to get my name on that list. Why else do you think we're in a hospital?"

The two goblins screwed up their faces. The silly pair didn't have a clue!

Jack Frost tutted. "With all these good little children about, scribbling on the scroll should be easy. No one will notice one extra name in a list that long!"

Angelica landed gently beside Kirsty. "No one can write their name on the enchanted scroll," she explained in a quiet whisper. "It appears by magic if you do something good."

Kirsty looked confused. "Why would

Jack Frost want his name on Santa's list of good children anyway?" she asked.

"Easy!" declared Rachel. "He's after an extra-big pile of presents this year!"

The friends watched as Jack Frost rolled up the scroll and stuck it back in his pocket.

"If I can't write on this old scrap, I'll find someone who can," said Jack Frost, his ice-cold eyes glinting with determination. "This place is crawling with doctors and nurses. All we've got to do is trick one of them into writing my name for me. Someone sickeningly good like them should get the magic going!"

The goblins started to chuckle.

"*Sick*-eningly good!" snorted one. "Nice joke for hospital, boss!"

The other clutched his belly and began to hoot with laughter.

Jack Frost didn't even crack a smile. Instead he grabbed both goblins by the scruff of the neck and yanked them down behind the bed.

"Someone's coming!" he hissed, ducking out of sight.

There was the sound of footsteps and the creak of a

door being pushed open.

"Oh no," gasped Kirsty. "It's the doctor we saw earlier!"

Three Poorly Patients

"Is anyone in here?" called the doctor, flicking on the main light. "This ward should be closed."

Jack Frost leapt out from behind the bed, hastily straightening his porter's coat.

"Just us hospital workers," he fibbed. "We're giving the place a Christmas clean. Got to keep it nice for the children, eh?"

The two goblins looked at each other

shiftily. Jack Frost shot them such a fierce glare they started clumsily making one of the beds. Angelica and her friends flitted up out of sight.

Jack Frost turned back to the doctor.

"I'm sure you got the memo," he insisted, pulling the enchanted scroll out of his pocket. "All you've got to do is sign here and we'll have this place looking tiptop for your next lot of patients."

The doctor looked uneasy.

"Hurry up," pressed one of the goblins. "We've got work to do."

Angelica covered her worried eyes.

"This isn't how the enchanted scroll should be treated," she sobbed. "I can't bear to look!"

Jack Frost handed the pen to the doctor. Kirsty and Rachel clutched Angelica's hands.

"I'll sign that form later," the doctor announced, taking the pen. "You three need a prescription first!"

Jack Frost's lip began to tremble.

"Wh-what's a prescription?" he stuttered.

The doctor pulled a pad out of his pocket. "It's a list of medicines I want you to take. I've never seen anyone so off-colour!"

Before they could argue, the cheeky

threesome found themselves being helped
into hospital beds. The doctor pushed a
thermometer into Jack
Frost's mouth, then
walked round
to examine
the goblins.
 "Say
'ahhh'!"
he muttered.
"You're

practically *green*. You must be feeling
terribly sick."

 "Now you come to mention it…"
groaned the goblin with the wonky nose,
his voice trailing off into a sob.

 "Help!" sniffed his mate. "Am I going
to make it, Doc?"

 Kirsty did a somersault on the spot.

"Jack Frost's plan is backfiring," she beamed.

"And now those silly goblins really believe that they're poorly," added Angelica, trying not to giggle.

Kirsty blinked with surprise as the doctor pulled the thermometer out of Jack Frost's mouth. There was a tinkly, splitting sound – the glass tube had frozen solid!

"That's impossible!" said the stunned doctor, rubbing his eyes and checking again. "How can it give me a minus reading? Let's get you wrapped up nice and warm."

Rachel tried not to giggle as the doctor

piled blankets and hot-water bottles into Jack Frost's bed. The Ice Lord's spiky hair and beard began to droop and his nose turned a funny shade of pink.

"I think I'm melting!" he wailed. "Stop it!"

Luckily this doctor was used to difficult

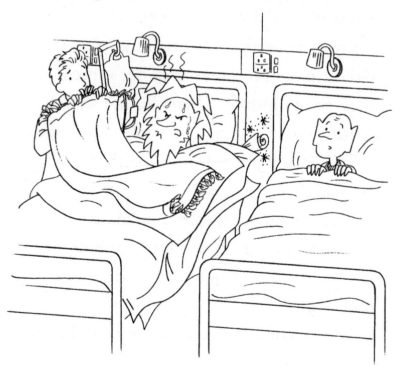

patients. He tucked all three in extra tight, telling them that they should be fine as long as they rested up for a week or two. By the time he headed back off on his rounds, the trio were feeling too rotten to argue.

"That's it, then," groaned one of the goblins, "Christmas is cancelled!"

Angelica pointed down to Jack Frost's bed – she could still see the enchanted scroll sticking out from under the bedcovers.

"Shall we fly down and get it?" she suggested.

Kirsty's eyes began to twinkle.

"I have an even better idea," she replied.

A Very Merry Christmas!

Kirsty took Rachel and Angelica's hands.

"If we can persuade Jack Frost to give the enchanted scroll back, his name might appear on the parchment all by itself," she whispered.

Angelica nodded. "That way Santa will remember to bring him some presents, too."

"Let's give Jack Frost a chance to do something good," agreed Rachel. "It is Christmas after all."

The friends darted out from their hiding spot.

As soon as they saw the trails of golden fairy dust shimmering above their beds, the goblins began to howl.

"Call the doctor back!" yelled the one with the crooked nose.

"I'm starting to see things!"

"Not 'things'," smiled Kirsty, "*fairies!*"

Angelica hovered over Jack Frost's bed.

"Please may

I have my enchanted scroll back?" she asked sweetly. "There's still enough time to make sure that the children here and all over the world get the Christmas presents they deserve."

Jack Frost stuck his tongue out. "No! What about the presents *I* deserve?"

Rachel plucked up all her courage, then fluttered a little closer.

"Don't be mean," she urged. "If you give the scroll back to Angelica you might see your name on Santa's list."

Jack Frost hesitated for a moment.

"That's right," she continued. "It only takes one good deed to make the magic work."

"Time is running out," called Kirsty. "It's now or never!"

Angelica held out both hands and waited patiently.

Jack Frost scowled, then pulled the scroll out from under the covers.

"All right," he grimaced. "Take the stupid thing!"

The instant the scroll left his hands, the parchment shrank back down to fairy-size.

"Thank you!" cooed the Angel Fairy, clutching the magical object to her chest.

Kirsty and Rachel watched spellbound as Angelica carefully undid the red velvet ribbon and unravelled the enchanted scroll. Even Jack Frost peeped nervously over his blankets.

Angelica ran her tiny fingertip down the list of names. There were thousands, each written with beautiful fountain pen. Her finger stopped halfway down the page.

"Here you are," she read carefully. "FROST, JACK."

The Ice Lord couldn't help but grin. He even pushed himself up in the bed and high-fived his goblins!

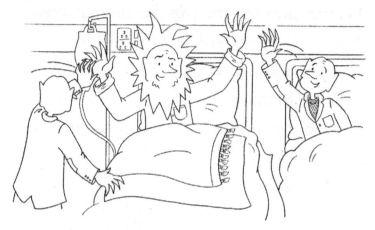

"It's time to go back to your Ice Castle," said Angelica, "but when you wake up tomorrow morning there might be a few surprises waiting for you!"

A fountain of glittering swirls cascaded out of Angelica's wand, bathing Jack Frost and his goblins in an exquisite golden light.

Jack Frost muttered something quietly.

"What was that?" asked Kirsty.

Jack Frost lifted his arms into the air, then summoned the two goblins to stand close.

"If you must know," he snapped, "I said, 'Merry Christmas'!"

There was a crack of lightning and the trio were gone.

"I never thought I'd hear Jack Frost talk like that," marvelled the Angel Fairy, rolling the scroll up and tucking it under her arm. "What a perfect end to our adventure together!"

"The adventure's not over quite yet," Kirsty reminded her. "You need to take the enchanted scroll to the North Pole. Santa will be waiting!"

At that moment, the lovely sound of children's laughter started to echo down the corridor.

"And we need to help the Brownies give out those presents," beamed Rachel.

"Let's hurry," added her best friend. "The children need to get to bed on time.

It *is* Christmas Eve!"

With a tap of her wand, Angelica changed Kirsty and Rachel back to their normal size.

"Goodbye," cried Rachel. "Merry Christmas!"

Angelica waved her magic wand one last time. A gorgeous rag doll with fairy wings suddenly appeared in Kirsty's outstretched hand. The doll had auburn hair and a frothy white dress, just like Angelica's!

"A special present," she winked. "For a little girl called Emily."

Lottie the Lollipop Fairy

Read on for a sneak peek...

"I can't *wait* for you to meet my Aunt Harri, Rachel!" Kirsty Tate exclaimed, beaming at her best friend, Rachel Walker. Rachel had arrived that morning to spend the spring half-term holiday with Kirsty in the pretty village of Wetherbury. "Mum's invited her to come to lunch today, so you'll be able to ask Aunt Harri all about *Candy Land*."

Rachel grinned. "I can't wait to meet Aunt Harri, either," she replied. "Working in a sweet factory must be one of the most wonderful jobs in the whole world!"

"I guess it's *almost* as wonderful as being

a fairy," Kirsty said, and the girls shared a secret smile. They'd had many thrilling adventures with their fairy friends and hoped to have lots more.

"The *Candy Land* factory is on a hill overlooking Wetherbury," Kirsty explained. "Aunt Harri gets lots of free sweets and she always brings a big bagful with her whenever she comes to visit."

"Oh, I'm looking forward to meeting her even more, then!" Rachel laughed.

There was a ring at the doorbell and the girls rushed to answer it. Outside stood a smiling, fair-haired young woman holding a bulging pink-and-white striped carrier bag. *Candy Land* was written across the side of the bag in sparkly silver glitter.

"Hello, Kirsty," Aunt Harri said, giving her a big hug. "And you must be Rachel." She hugged Rachel, too. "I've heard so much about you from Kirsty."

"I've heard lots about you, too," Rachel replied, smiling back.

"Then I'm sure Kirsty's told you all about *Candy Land*!" Aunt Harri said, her big blue eyes twinkling. "I thought you might like to try some of our sweets." And she handed the bag to the girls.

Eagerly, Rachel and Kirsty peeked inside. They could see lollipops, chocolate bars, and piles of other sweets wrapped in shiny coloured paper. However, to their dismay, the sweets looked broken and battered and not at all appetising. But, most unexpected of all, there was a horrible smell inside the bag that made both girls gasp and draw back slightly.

What on earth is that smell? Rachel thought, trying not to wrinkle up her nose in disgust. The sweets looked and smelt like rotting rubbish! But she didn't want to be rude and complain when Aunt Harri had been kind enough to bring them the sweets. Kirsty, too, was trying to smile politely at her aunt.

"Maybe we should wait until after lunch to try them," Kirsty suggested, closing the bag quickly.

Aunt Harri's face fell. "The sweets are really bad, aren't they?" she sighed. "Girls, something's gone terribly wrong at *Candy Land*. All the sweets look, smell and taste absolutely horrid!"

Read Lottie the Lollipop Fairy to find out what adventures are in store for Kirsty and Rachel!

Meet the fairies, play games
and get sneak peeks at
the latest books!

www.rainbowmagicbooks.co.uk

There's fairy fun for everyone on
our wonderful website.
You'll find great activities, competitions, stories and
fairy profiles, and also a special newsletter.

Get 30% off all Rainbow Magic books at

www.rainbowmagicbooks.co.uk

Enter the code RAINBOW at the checkout.
Offer ends 31 December 2013.

Offer valid in United Kingdom and Republic of Ireland only.

Competition!

Angelica the Angel Fairy has created this special crossword just for you! Read the clues and put the correct answers in the grid below. When you have all four answers, go online and enter!

CLUES

Down

1. One of Angelica's magical items is an

_ _ _ _ _ _ _ _ _ scroll

3. Complete this: Angelica the

_ _ _ _ _ Fairy

Across

2. This magical item belonging to Angelica is a snow-white _ _ _ _ _ _ _

4. Which fairy takes Kirsty and Rachel to meet Angelica in Fairyland? _ _ _ _ _ _ _

We will put all the correct entries into a draw and select a winner to receive a special Rainbow Magic Goodie Bag featuring lots of treats for you and your fairy friends.
You'll also star in a new Rainbow Magic story!

Enter online now at www.rainbowmagicbooks.co.uk

Meet the Sweet Fairies

Out April 2013!

Kirsty and Rachel must help the Sweet Fairies get
their magical charms back from Jack Frost – before
he ruins all sweet treats, for ever!

www.rainbowmagicbooks.co.uk